The Story of DAPHNE the Duck

Written and illustrated
by
Maxine E. Schreiber

MW01485354

The Story of DAPHNE the Duck

Story and illustrations

Copyright © 2014
by
Maxine E. Schreiber

All rights reserved
No duplication without written permission

This book is dedicated to my sister Janet Schreiber, who is my biggest supporter; my dear friends Jane Bonk Thomson, Debbie Goldman, Susan Stechnij, Mina Boniface, and Han Young, who always encourage me; Wendy Pottinger, Pamela Carey, Ruth Berge, Lisa Combs, and Karen Bain, the wonderful women of the Winers and Diners Writing Group; and John Vincent Palozzi, an artist/poet who taught me how to use Photoshop Elements and convinced me to self-publish.

ISBN-13:
978-1496148766

ISBN-10:
1496148762

Printed by CreateSpace, An Amazon.com Company

Published by Schreiber Studio
maxine@schreiberstudio.com
www.schreiberstudio.com

ABOUT THE STORY

One day in the summer of 2013, my sister told me that she noticed a hole in the middle of my potted garden on our fifth floor balcony. A hole? I wondered what she was talking about. The large pot was filled with hot pink pentas, yellow lantana, and wandering purple hearts. Sure enough when I went out to water my plants I noticed that in the center of the pot there was a small clearing as if a critter had dug out some of the flowers. I didn't think a lizard would do that, and I couldn't figure out what other creature might have been there. But since there were only flowers in the pot, I decided to go to Home Depot and buy a new penta to fill the space. I planted it that afternoon.

Two days later when I went out to water the new plant, I discovered an egg in the middle of the pot. I took a picture of it and wrote on Facebook asking what kind of bird lays an egg and flies away. The answer was a duck! The next day I purposely set my alarm to wake up at sunrise. It was just getting light out when I sat in my living room looking out at the potted garden. I was rewarded when a Muscovy duck flew on to the railing, and with a quack she jumped into the pot.

Muscovy ducks have been introduced to urban and suburban areas in Florida, but they are not native to the state and are considered a nuisance. Federal regulations prohibit their release into the wild because of their potential to transmit diseases or interbreed with Florida's native waterfowl. Perhaps because of this fact or because some people find them ugly, Muscovy ducks have been mistreated, abused, and maligned. I spent my summer watching Daphne each day, and she inspired me to tell her story. I'm hoping it will stimulate understanding and compassion for these lovable creatures.

ABOUT THE AUTHOR/ILLUSTRATOR

Maxine E. Schreiber closed her private psychotherapy practice to become a full-time professional artist and author. Her paintings have been exhibited in numerous galleries and museums and can be seen in her book *The Schreibers The Apple Doesn't Fall Far From the Tree.* An adult and young adult novelist, this is her first picture book. She is delighted that it has offered her the opportunity to express herself as both an illustrator and a writer. She lives in West Palm Beach, Florida.

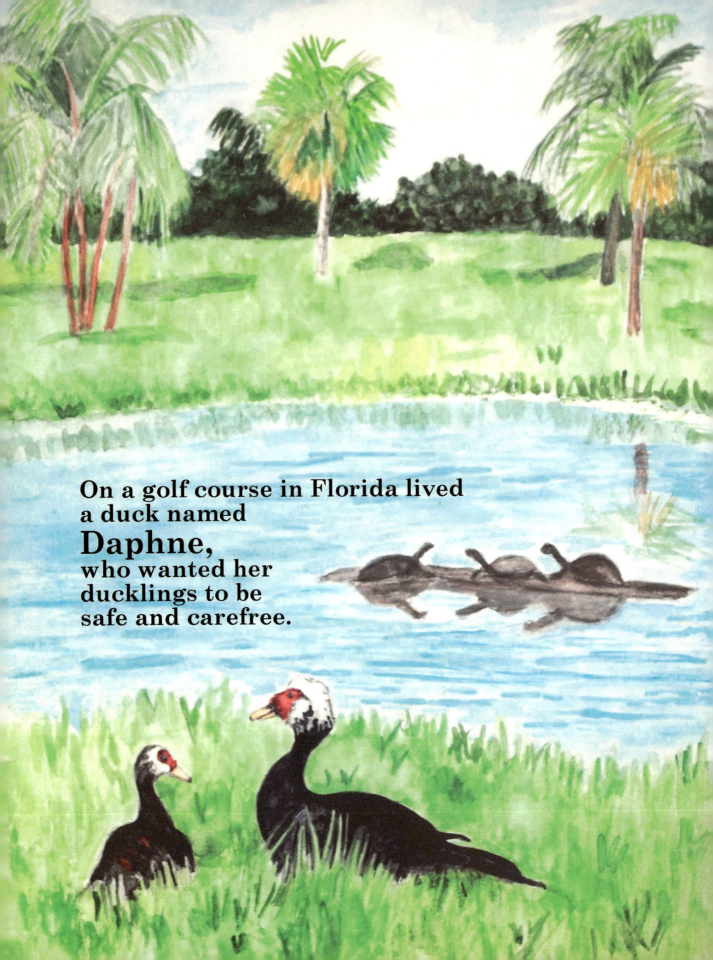

On a golf course in Florida lived
a duck named
Daphne,
who wanted her
ducklings to be
safe and carefree.

But the pond where she lived
had monsters galore -
egg eating turtles and a gator
for sure!

One day when
she flew past
the building
nearby,
she sighted a
flowerpot five
stories high.

The colorful
flowers,
bright
purple and
pink
caused her
to stop, to
look, and to
think.

On the railing where she landed to stop and to stare,
she couldn't see her mate,
Drake Muscovy, from there.

It scared her to think she was so far away,
but the terracotta pot convinced her to stay.

She jumped off the railing right into the dirt
thinking, I'll sit for awhile,
that can't really hurt.

But in the rich soil she laid one egg
before she flew to the pond to tell
her mate, **Drake.**

When she saw him
and told him, he
made a huge sigh.

Then he quacked
and he quacked,
**"I'm too big to fly
that far and
so high!"**

"I know," quacked Daphne, "I know that's true.

But our eggs will be safe there, so what can I do?"

She
returned
to the pot
the very
next day
and sat in
the dirt
the very
same way.

And the
day after
that,
on three
eggs
she
sat.

Each day she
returned to
sit in her
nest,
and after
twelve days
she decided
to rest.

Twelve eggs,
she thought.
This number
is fine.
She flew off
to the pond
to see
Drake
and to
dine.

The weeks that followed she sat each day,
and as the weeks passed the longer
she'd stay.

One day a crow came and scared her a lot.
It strutted and cawed,

"What's in that pot?"

Daphne raised her head feathers
and stuck out her chest.
Though scared as can be,
she protected her nest.

She sighed with relief when the crow flew away and decided to feather the nest that day.

She took small, fuzzy feathers from under a wing and covered each egg, covered every last thing.

"Better safe than sorry," she quacked
on her flight
as she went to the pond that
very same night.

And she felt more secure with her eggs
hidden from sight.

The next afternoon she took a short break
to visit the pond and have time with Drake.

But she missed the twelve eggs when she was away.
So later that night at the pot she did stay.

No more nights at
the pond. Her nights
would be here -
alone with the twelve
eggs in the pot that
they shared.

She thought of the
future and how happy
they would be -
on the pond -
their daddy,
the twelve
ducklings, and she!

Her time on the
balcony grew
*longer and
longer,* and the
time at the pond
grew *shorter
and shorter.*

Long lonely
days she sat in
the pot
with the sun
beating down
making her
hot!

Until the day she heard
a loud crack
and felt something move
from her front to her back.

The first one that hatched
all cuddly and small
popped out in front
and stood very tall.

She looked at
his eagerness
to see and to be
and decided
to name
this duckling
QUICKY.

When he got
sleepy and
nestled at her
breast,
she patiently
waited to meet
the rest.

One by one each duckling came forth.
First **Fuzzy,** then **Downy,** and **Fluffy**
were born.

By the end of the day, two more
cracked their shells.
Plucky and **Lucky,** but that didn't
make twelve.

Six little ducklings peeped, and they peeped.
They scurried and climbed,
stepped on each other, and hid by her side.

Not all the eggs cracked. There were a dozen in all,
but only six ducklings were finally born.
All night they cheeped, and all night they scampered.

She would have liked twelve, but six were a handful.

The very next morning when the
sun finally rose,
she jumped from the pot and
stood on her toes.

From the balcony floor she
quacked to her brood,

"Ducklings, please hurry. There's no time to lose.
I've been gone for so long, and your dad is alone.
It's time to head to the pond.
It's time to go home!"

The ducklings climbed, and the
ducklings clambered.
One by one they jumped and one
by one they landed.

"Follow me," she quacked when
  their feet reached the floor.
"Follow me, follow me, and
  you'll learn how to soar."

She raced across the floor with the
ducklings at her heels.
Then she pushed her way through
the balcony rails.

She flew to the ground excited to see
that the ducklings all jumped,
and they all flapped their wings.

All landed on the ground not far from their mom,
a pile of brown fluff that seemed unharmed.

But then she saw it, a really scary thing.
A cat was stalking her tiny ducklings!

With its eyes on her, it slunk to the ground
and crept toward them with a sinister frown.

Then a little girl rushed out and scooped up the **cat,** and the **danger ended just like that!**

When the ducklings sprang to
their feet and stood in a row,
Daphne sighed with relief and
quacked, **"Let's go!"**

She headed the line
through the tall grass
with the six
little ducklings
following
fast.

In the habit of flying back
and forth each day,
the trek on webbed feet
was a much harder way.

But the
ducklings
needed to learn
how to walk,
so she stopped
now and then to
rest and to talk.

"I'm eager to see
your father,"
she quacked.
"So we'll
   continue
     this
      march
  until
     we're
       all
         the
      way
         back."

She saw him waiting his face covered with glee as she returned with their family.

The work was cut out for her and for Drake to keep their six ducklings happy and safe.

Six ducklings in all, six ducklings to feed, they all reached the pond.
What else could she need?

31477818R00024

Made in the USA
Lexington, KY
13 April 2014